Chasing Rainbows

Gabby Grant

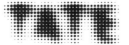

TATE

It was a miserable day. It was raining when Emmy woke up, and it was STILL raining after lunch.

"It's horrible. The whole day feels grey," she sighed.

"I know," said Dad, "but we need the rain as well as the sun. It helps the flowers to grow."

"I wish there was just a tiny bit of sun," said Emmy. "Maybe I'd see a rainbow!"

"OK misery-chops," said Dad. "We'll have to find our own. Grab your raincoat and let's go chase a rainbow!"

Emmy had never chased a rainbow before, but it sounded like more fun than sitting indoors.

They ventured outside into the rain. Emmy tried to kick up some leaves on the ground, but they went "squish" instead of "crunch" and she scowled down at them stuck to her wellies.

"Wait, I think I've found a trail!" said Dad. "You know how an animal's paw prints can show you where they have been? Well, rainbows leave colours behind them."

He showed her a red leaf, then a yellow one. "This means our rainbow has been along here."

Emmy looked down again, and picked up a leaf that was bright orange. "Ooh," said Dad excitedly.

"That proves it was here only moments ago!"

There was a whoosh of noise behind them.

"Was that the rainbow?" asked Emmy.

"It looked like some cyclists," replied Dad.
"But do you think . . . ?"

"It's hiding behind them?!"
yelled Emmy excitedly.

They chased after it
and found where it
had zigged between
the swings . . .

and zagged through
the climbing frame . . .

and skidded
down the slide.

Emmy wasn't sure if it had gone on the roundabout, but she checked anyway because roundabouts were her favourite thing.

They had a few clues and Emmy was on the look out for more.

"Do you think it went past those houses?" she asked.

"It looks like it knocked on that door," Dad replied.

"Maybe it asked for a drink and a biscuit?" said Emmy.

"Well, I hope it said 'please'!" laughed Dad.

The more Emmy looked, the more colours she found!
She spotted where the rainbow had sniffed at a wall . . .

where it had left its footprints in a garden and
even where it had scratched its bottom on a van!

"I think it's hiding in the corner shop!" Dad called, and they both rushed over to see.

But when they got there, all they could find were posters and comics.

"Oh no!" cried Emmy.
"I thought we'd found it."

"It only just got away,"
said Dad. "Maybe it's
heading to the high street?"

"Quick, let's go!" shouted Emmy,
and they were off on the rainbow's
trail once again.

Emmy KNEW they were catching up with the rainbow now.

She could see where its tail had brushed
against people's clothes and hair.

Its giant paws had splashed in the puddles and left bright wiggles of colour, and its eye seemed to wink from the reflections in the windows.

"There it is!" cheered Emmy, as the rainbow
sneaked through a flower shop window.

But the rainbow swished on through the greengrocer's next door and it was gone again.

Emmy wanted to keep on searching for the rainbow, but Dad said, "It's hard work chasing rainbows. I think intrepid hunters like us need a refreshment break."

Dad bought Emmy a biscuit and a strawberry milkshake with colourful sprinkles on the top.

"I think the rainbow must have sneezed on it!" said Dad.

"Eurgh, Dad!" said Emmy giggling, but she drank it all the same. It was delicious!

As the rainbow chasers headed home, Dad said, "I'm sorry we didn't catch the rainbow, Emmy."

"It's OK," said Emmy. "Chasing the rainbow was fun, and I know we'll catch it next time!"

She skipped and splashed through the puddles towards home. It was still raining, but the sky seemed just a bit brighter.

And then, just as they turned the corner and arrived back at home, Emmy looked up . . .

"Wow!" she gasped.

Their beautiful rainbow, wrapping a

colourful ribbon around the clouds,

just for her!

A few moments later, the rain stopped and the rainbow slipped away . . . but where to?

To Hannah, and to everyone at Tate Publishing,
for not stopping believing, as the song almost says.

Thank you for putting so much time and care into this book,
despite working through strange times. I also appreciate the
kindness with which you answered all my daft questions.

And love to all my family who've cheered me on over the years
(with a special mention to Connie and her inspirational hair). xx

First published 2021 by order of the Tate Trustees by Tate Publishing,
a division of Tate Enterprises Ltd, Millbank, London SW1P 4RG
www.tate.org.uk/publishing

Text and illustrations © 2021 Gabby Grant

ISBN 978 1 84976 760 6

Distributed in the United States and Canada by ABRAMS, New York

Library of Congress Control Number applied for

Colour reproduction by Evergreen Colour Management Ltd
Printed and bound in China by C&C Offset Printing Co., Ltd